For Laura and Clara – PR

A Letter to Grandma

Paul Rogers · John Prater

ATHENEUM   1994   NEW YORK

Maxwell Macmillan International
New York   Oxford   Singapore   Sydney

Atheneum
Macmillan Publishing Company
866 Third Avenue
New York, NY 10022

Macmillan Publishing Company is part of
the Maxwell Communication Group of Companies.

First U.S. edition

Originally published in Great Britain by The Bodley Head Children's Books.

Printed in Hong Kong

10 9 8 7 6 5 4 3 2 1

ISBN 0 689 31947 9

Lucy lay in her bed, in her room, in her house, on Maple Street, and thought of the whole town spread out around her.

She fell asleep listening to night noises – distant cars and dogs barking into the dark – and thinking about tomorrow, when Grandma would come.

The moment she woke, she knew
something was different. Where had all
the houses gone? The streets? The town?
From her window she could see nothing
but sea!

She ran out of the house, barefoot
onto the sand – past the yard, past the
garage, past the front door, under her
own bedroom window.

"Breakfast's ready!" Mom called.

Lucy climbed back up the cliff, leaving
a necklace of footprints around the island.

"The mailman's late," said Dad.

"I guess the traffic's bad," said Mom.

"I'm going out to watch the whales,"
said Lucy.

That's where my school used to be, she thought, over there. This is where the street was. She picked up a starfish. "And there," she laughed as two crabs scuttled away, "that's where Mr. and Mrs. Horner lived."

At lunchtime Lucy told Mom and Dad all about the rock pools, the fish, and the sea. But they didn't seem to be listening.

During dessert there was a knock at the door.
"I'll go!" Lucy said.

An enormous liner was anchored off the front yard. On the porch stood its captain. "Excuse me," he said. "I think we're lost. I can't figure out where I am."

"This is 101 Maple Street," said Lucy.

"Ah, thank you," said the captain. "Sorry to bother you."

After lunch Lucy's parents worked in the yard.
"Look at these lupines!" complained Mom.

"Look at those dolphins!" called Lucy from the beach.

Suddenly she remembered Grandma.
How would she ever get here now?
Someone would have to tell her!
At her toes Lucy saw an old bottle.
She hurried indoors for pen and
paper and wrote:

Dear Grandma,
I can't wait to see you.
Our new address is
101 Maple Street Island.
Please come soon.
Love from Lucy

Then rolling the message up, she
slipped it into the bottle and pushed
it out to sea.

That was when Lucy felt the first drops of rain. The sky grew dark, the sea grew wild, and soon Lucy was hurrying to the house for shelter. From the window she watched the storm.

Now Grandma will never make it, she thought.

Then, way out in the distance, she spotted a small boat. One moment it was riding a giant wave, the next it was lost from sight. But gradually it grew bigger and bigger until Lucy could make out her Grandma, waving.

"Hello, Grandma!" she called, running to the water's edge. The rain stopped, and together they climbed the path to the house.

"You look a bit wet," said Dad. "Did you have to wait for the bus?"

After supper Lucy took Grandma on a tour of the island. She showed her the crabs and gulls, the rock pools and starfish.

"Look," said Grandma, "I've got something for you. Hold it to your ear. What do you hear?"

So Lucy pressed the warm-colored, soft-looking, cold, hard shell to her ear. And in it she heard the sound of the sea.

Then she sat on Grandma's lap, on the deck chair, on the beach, on the island, and together they watched the ripe sun going down.

When it was time for Grandma to go, Lucy waved her good-bye from the gate. She watched her climbing into the boat and sailing slowly, slowly away.

"Time for bed," said Dad.

"I guess Grandma will steer by the stars," said Lucy.

That night Lucy fell asleep listening to the
sighing of the sea and dreamed all about . . .

. . . tomorrow.

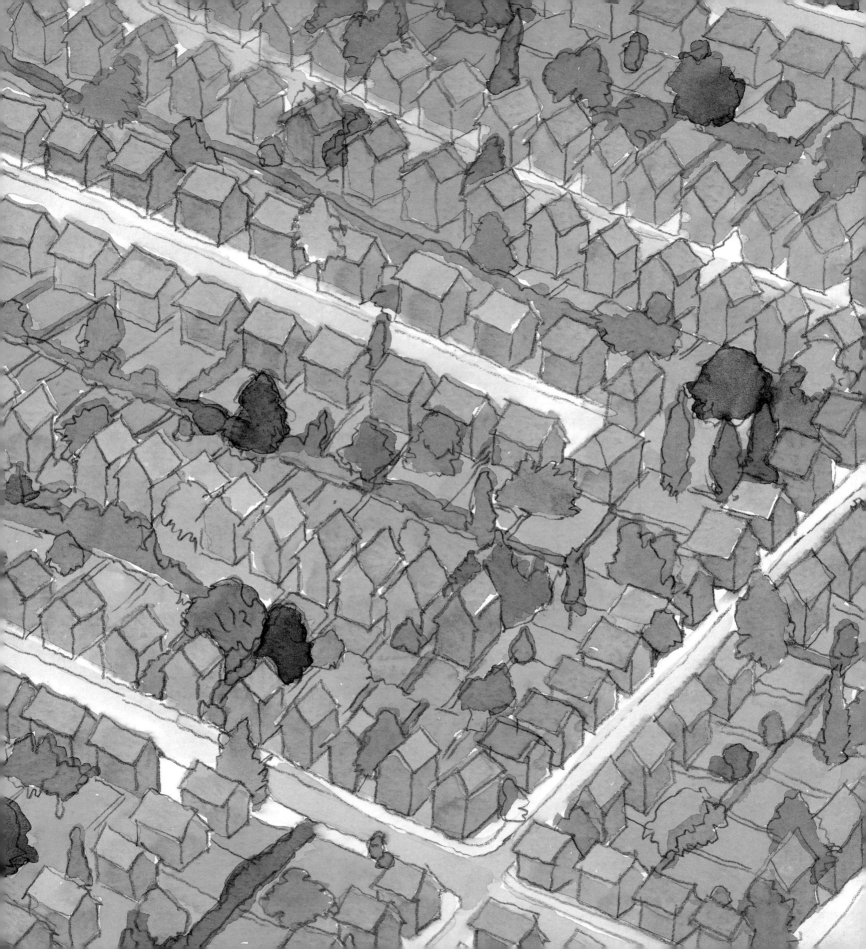